This book belongs to

..................................................

..................................................

The friends
Peter the Penguin
Pom the Panda

Benny the Cat    Teddy the Bear

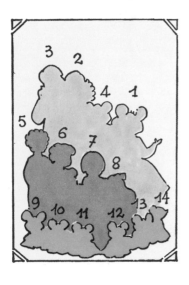

1. Mary Mouse
2. Mummy Doll
3. Daddy Doll
4. Whiskers Mouse
5. Pip
6. Melia
7. Roundy
8. Jumpy
9. Woffly
10. Scamper
11. Patter
12. Squeaker
13. Tiny
14. Frisky

# The adventures of Mary Mouse

Enid Blyton

## ℛℛ
RAVETTE BOOKS

Printed and bound for Ravette Books Limited,
3 Glenside Estate, Star Road
Partridge Green, Horsham
West Sussex RH13 8RA
An Egmont Company
in Great Britain

ISBN: 1 85304 347 8

# Contents

# Chapter 1

# Introducing Mary Mouse

Somewhere in France there is a big house where children used to play long ago. Now they have gone and their toys have been put away.

But if you go upstairs to the attic and over to the far corner, under the eaves, you will find a dear little Doll's House, built of strong red bricks. It has a dark brown roof, one chimney and a garden with flowers all around.

Perhaps you will stop and knock at the door to see if anyone is at home. Who do you think will greet you? A doll! No, you are wrong! When the door opens, you will see a little grey head, a pointed nose, some fine whiskers and two little round ears. Yes, it is a mouse. But this is no ordinary mouse. For she is wearing a blouse covered with flowers, and a crisp white apron on top of a black skirt. The name of this mouse is Mary. Mary Mouse.

Mary Mouse lives in the Doll's House with the Doll family. There is Daddy Doll. He used to be a sailor. He has blonde hair and a blonde moustache. Then there is Mummy Doll, who is dark and pretty. And there are three children, who are blonde like their father. Their names are Melia, Pip and Roundy. There is Roundy peeping through the window!

Mary Mouse works very hard. From morning to night she scampers all over the house sweeping, dusting, cooking, washing up and mending clothes. Each day she goes out with a basket to do the shopping and she looks after all the Doll family. She finds Daddy Doll's pipe when he loses it. She makes lovely dresses for Mummy Doll and she cares for the children.

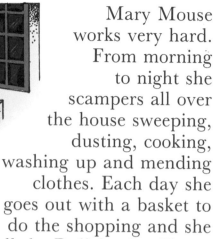

Poor Mummy Doll: she is not very well. She needs to rest a lot,

and she cannot look after the house
like Mary does. And the children
make her very tired, especially when
Pip is naughty and slides down the
banisters.

The children love Mary Mouse.
She scolds them when they are
naughty and puts them to bed at
night when they are tired. And when
Roundy falls down, she picks him up
and bathes his hurt knees.

Sometimes Mary Mouse makes a beautiful cake for the family and writes on it with icing. I wonder what she writes!

At night Mary is so tired that she goes to bed early, in her little room at the top of the Doll's House.

"I am so happy," she says, as she closes her eyes and goes fast asleep.

Sleep well, Mary Mouse!

## Chapter 2

# Melia's Birthday Party

It was soon to be Melia's birthday. "I am going to be five years old," she said. "Please Mummy! May I have a party?" Mummy Doll spoke to Mary Mouse.

"Of course you must have a party," said Mary. "You shall have a lovely party." So that afternoon Mary went out and invited all Melia's friends. There was Peter the Penguin. And Teddy the Bear. And

Pom the Panda. And last of all,
Benny the Toy Cat.

Then Mary Mouse went home to
make all the sandwiches and cakes
and jellies for tea. She lit the fire to
make the oven hot.
Oh, dear! It went out
again. Mary tried
again, but this time
a thick black cloud
of smoke billowed
out of the stove.
Mary was
alarmed.

"I must go
and get the
chimney sweep,"

she said. And she put on her hat and out she went.

Pip thought it would be great fun to sweep the chimney. So he ran off and found a broom and poked it right up the kitchen chimney. But, oh dear! An enormous lump of soot fell down on top of him! That made him look just like a chimney sweep!

At that moment Melia came into the kitchen.

"Help! Help! A robber!" she cried, seeing a strange sooty person in front of her. Daddy Doll picked up a stick and ran to chase the robber away. Pip ran out of the house crying, and bumped straight into Mary Mouse and knocked her over.

"You bad boy," said Mary. "I will have to take you upstairs and give you a bath." Soon the real sweep came with his brushes and poles. He fitted the poles together and put the brushes on the top. Melia and

Roundy went outside and there was
a brush coming out of the chimney!

"The chimney is alright now,"
said the sweep. "You can bake your
cakes."

Mary mixed the eggs and flour
and sugar together and put the
mixture in the oven. Soon she had
sandwiches and jellies and cakes
ready to go on the table. And best of
all, there was a wonderful birthday

cake with five layers and five candles on the top. It was decorated with pink icing.

Mary helped the children to dress. Pip and Roundy wore blue trousers and Melia had a new dress. Mummy

and Daddy Doll dressed up too; and Mary Mouse put on a clean white apron.

Then the guests began to arrive. Teddy the Bear came first, then Peter the Penguin. Pom the Panda and Benny the Toy Cat came together. They all brought presents for Melia.

"Happy birthday, Melia," they

said. "Happy birthday!"

"Thank you," said Melia.

Everyone sat down to tea. Teddy the Bear ate sixteen cakes, fourteen sandwiches and two jellies. His tummy got so fat that a button popped right off his new coat. After that he didn't dare to eat any more.

Mary lit the five candles on the birthday cake.

"Happy birthday, dear Melia," everybody sang.

When Melia cut the cake, she gave the biggest piece of all to Mary. Then they pulled the crackers. Roundy liked the bangs. Melia got a red hat, Pip had a mauve one with a moon on it and Roundy had a little green one.

Next they played games. Pip caught Mary in Blind Man's Buff. Of course he guessed who it was! Pom the Panda won Hunt the Thimble. Mary had hidden it on top of Roundy's head. He had to sit very still while everyone was looking.

At the end they all had a turn at fishing for parcels, which Daddy Doll had hidden in a big barrel. Even Mary had a turn. She got a big red parcel.

"Go on! Open it Mary!" everyone said. Inside was a beautiful pair of warm slippers. Mary was very pleased.

Then it was time for the guests to go home. They all said goodbye and thank you for a lovely time.

Mary put the three tired children to bed.

"Thank you, thank you, Mary Mouse," said Melia. "That was the

best birthday party I ever had!" She hugged Mary hard.

Mary washed up and cleaned the kitchen and the living room. And then she went to bed feeling very happy indeed.

## Chapter 3

# The Family Go on Holiday

A few days after Melia's birthday, Daddy Doll said,

"It is going to get hot soon. Let's go on holiday to the sea."

Melia, Pip and Roundy were very excited.

"I shall catch a fish," said Pip.

"I shall swim," said Melia.

"What is the sea?" said Roundy.

Mary ran upstairs into the bedrooms and got all the suitcases.

"Melia's dress, Pip's bathing
trunks, Mummy Doll's sun hat,
Daddy Doll's binoculars," she said
to herself as she went.

"Now my sunshade, my knitting
to keep myself busy while I watch
the children . . . Let me see. Let me
see. Have I forgotten anything?"

Mary Mouse was so busy that she
did not see Roundy coming up the

stairs. Roundy peeped into a big trunk to see what was inside. Suddenly he fell in. He liked being inside the trunk and hid under some clothes. The clothes were nice and warm and soon Roundy fell asleep. Mary finished the packing and shut the cases and the big trunk. Click! Click! Click!

Soon it was lunch time and Mary called Roundy. There was no reply. Roundy had vanished! Nobody had seen him at all. Melia looked in the wardrobe. Pip looked in the toy cupboard. Daddy Doll went into the garden and shouted,

"Roundy! Roundy! Where are you?" Still there was no reply. Mummy Doll began to cry.

Suddenly Roundy woke up and cried. No one knew where the sound was coming from. At last Mary opened the cases and out of the big trunk climbed Roundy.

"My poor darling Roundy!" said
Mummy Doll.

The time came to start their
journey. All the family went to the
station to catch the clockwork train.
Chuff, chuff, chuff! Here it comes

into the station! Everyone got in very excited.

The journey was a long one and Melia, Pip and Roundy got tired of sitting still. So Mary told them a story. The story was about Mary Mouse herself.

"Once upon a time," said Mary, "I lived down a mouse hole with my mother and father and four brothers and sisters."

"What were their names?" asked Melia.

"Morris, Michael, Maud and Marigold," said Mary. "And I was the youngest. My mother and father were always cross with me," said Mary. "And my brothers and sisters teased me."

"Why were they cross?" asked Roundy.

"Because I was so tidy," said Mary. "Mother and Father liked to live in a dirty and untidy house.

'Don't fuss so,' they said. But I couldn't stop cleaning and tidying. So one day they turned me out of the mouse hole. 'We don't want you here any more,' they said. 'Go away and clean someone else's house.' So I packed my suitcase and went away."

"Poor Mary Mouse," said Melia. "What did you do next?"

"I walked a long way, until I came to a beautiful little house made of red bricks, with a brown roof and a garden full of flowers."

"That's our house!" cried Pip in excitement.

"Was it our house, Mary?" asked Melia, taking Mary's paw.

"Shh!" said Mary. "You must wait while I tell the story."

"First I knocked on the door. But no one came. So I looked through the windows. The house was quite empty. So I went in. There were five rooms inside — a kitchen, a living room and three bedrooms. And they all wanted a good clean," said Mary. "So I found a long brush and swept the cobwebs off the ceiling. And I swept the floors well and scrubbed the kitchen floor. I shook the dust out of all the mats. Then I made some little cakes and put them in the oven."

"And then what happened?" asked Melia.

"I was very tired," said Mary. "So I crept upstairs and into one of the beds and went fast asleep. And when I woke up Mummy and Daddy Doll

were standing beside the bed."

"I knew it! I knew it!" cried Pip, jumping up and down on the seat. "Were they cross with you?"

"Oh no!" said Mary. "They were so pleased that I had cleaned the house that they

asked me to stay with
you always. That is
why I am here now."

"I love you, Mary
Mouse!" said Roundy.
And he went to sleep leaning
against her.

Soon the train came to
the end of the line.

"Here is our station!"
said Daddy Doll. "Let us get
out. Our holiday has begun!"

Chapter 4

# The Seaside

As soon as the Doll family and Mary Mouse left the train, Mummy and Daddy Doll went to look at the house where they were to stay. Mary Mouse took the children to the sea.

"What a big bath!" said Roundy.

The holiday passed happily. Pip, Melia and Roundy paddled in the sea. Melia and Pip caught shrimps in their big nets. Roundy sat down in a pool with all his clothes on. Sometimes they built big sandcastles, while Mary sat underneath her sunshade and knitted as she watched them.

One day Mary was very tired. So she lay down and went to sleep. Pip and Melia covered her with sand very quietly and she did not wake. Then the children went away to paddle in the sea. Soon Mary woke up and shook off all the sand. She went off to buy ice creams for everyone.

Suddenly a big crab, hiding in the sand, pinched Roundy's toe. He cried and cried. Melia took him to find Mary, but she couldn't find where they had buried her. Melia was very frightened. Pip was frightened too. They hunted all over the beach and dug a big hole where they thought Mary was buried. Some people on the beach looked for her

too. Even the donkeys helped.

Then they saw Mary walking across the sand, carrying ice creams. "Mary! Mary!" they shouted. "We thought we had lost you."

"Sit down and eat your ice creams," said Mary.

"Don't go away again," said Roundy. "I don't like crabs."

One morning Daddy Doll took
everyone out in a big rowing boat.
Daddy Doll rowed and Pip sat in the
bow with the fishing rod and tried
to catch a fish. He caught a big one.
But it was so big that it swam away
with the line, and the rod, and with
poor Pip too. Into the sea he went
with a splash, still holding the rod.

Brave Mary Mouse dived into the
water after him. Splash! She swam
to Pip and caught him by his jersey.
He was so frightened. Daddy Doll
pulled them both back into
the boat.

"How brave
you are,
Mary,"

38

"How brave you are, Mary,"
he said. "You shall have a medal!"

The very next day Melia, Pip and
Roundy all had swimming lessons,
in case they fell in again.

## Chapter 5

# Mary Mouse and the Burglar

At last
the
holiday
by the sea
came to an end. Mary Mouse
packed the suitcases and the family
caught the train back home. It was
lovely to see the little Doll's House
again.

Daddy Doll unlocked the door. Oh
dear! What a shock! Burglars had
been there. Everything was upside

down and many things had been stolen.

Mary Mouse put on her hat and went down to the police station. The policeman came to the house and made a list of everything that had been stolen. What a long list!

One sailor's hat, he wrote, one pink lamp, two shiny saucepans, a curly-haired doll, two books, one big blue brooch. Oh dear! When he had finished, there was no lead left in his pencil!

But it was Mary Mouse who found the burglar. Soon after the policeman left, she went out shopping with her basket. On her way she met Zephyr, the toy monkey.

"Good morning," she said.

Then she stopped. Good gracious! Zephyr was wearing Daddy Doll's sailor's hat on his head. Very quietly Mary Mouse followed Zephyr to his

house and looked through the window. And there she saw, on the table, the pink lamp, two shiny saucepans, a curly-haired doll, two books and a big blue brooch.

Mary ran back to the policeman.

"Come quickly," she said. "I have found the burglar."

The policeman put on his hat and followed Mary Mouse to Zephyr's house. He hammered on the door loudly. But the monkey did not want to open it.

"Open the door! Open the door!"

shouted the policeman fiercely.

At last Zephyr opened the door and in went Mary and the policeman and found all the stolen goods. The policeman took Zephyr to the police station, and Mary went home and told all the Doll family.

Pip took the wheelbarrow and wheeled all the stolen goods back to the Doll's House. Everyone was delighted. Melia made a cake and wrote in icing on the top: *For Mary Mouse the Detective.*

# Chapter 6

# Mary
# and the Black Cat

One day Melia was very naughty.
Mary had told her that she must
never play with a ball in the house.
But Melia fetched her ball and
began to play with it in the living
room. Crash! The ball knocked over
Mummy Doll's pink lamp and it fell
to the floor and broke.

Mummy Doll was very upset.

"I have no money to buy a new one," she said. Melia began to cry and ran to tell Mary.

"You are a naughty girl," said Mary. "How many times have I told you not to play ball in the house?"

"Please Mary," said Melia. "How can I get some money to buy Mummy a new lamp?"

Mary Mouse found some jobs for Melia to do. She took the next door baby for a walk. She ran errands for Pom the Panda and she mended Benny the Toy Cat's sock. She put the pennies in her money box. Soon there were enough to buy Mummy Doll another lamp.

Melia and Mary Mouse went to the shop to buy a new lamp. They found a very pretty one. Melia carried it carefully out of the shop and down the road. But then a dreadful thing happened.

They met a big black cat waiting

at the corner. The cat
pounced on
Mary and held
her under his
paw.

"Here is a nice
dinner for me!"
he said. Mary
squealed loudly.

"Let me go!
Let me go!"
Melia dropped the lamp and ran
home.

"Daddy, Daddy!"
she cried. "Come
and save Mary."
Daddy and
Mummy Doll
rushed
up. But the cat was
much bigger than
they were.

"Call the
policeman!" cried

Mummy Doll. But the cat was much bigger than the policeman too.

Then Daddy had a good idea. He went up behind the cat and he barked loudly, like a dog.

"Woof Woof Woof! Grrrr." The cat sprang away in fright, and set Mary Mouse free. Poor Mary tried to get up, but her leg was hurt and she couldn't walk at all.

So Daddy Doll picked her up and carried her home, and the family put her to bed. Mummy Doll made her a nice cup of tea. Pip brought her a new book to read. Melia went out and bought some sweets for her. And Roundy gave her his best train. Mary was very pleased.

"I am sorry, Mary," said Melia. "It was my fault you were attacked. It was because I was naughty and broke the lamp. And now the new lamp is broken too. I will never be naughty again."

At last Mary was better and came downstairs to see everyone. Mummy Doll had made a wonderful cake for her and across the top of the cake

she had written: *Welcome downstairs again Mary*.

Mary took Melia by the hand.

"As soon as we have some money, we are going out again to buy

Mummy another lamp. And this
time we shall bring it home safely."
And so they did.

## Chapter 7

# Mary Mouse Goes Away

Soon Mary was quite better. But the children did not go on being good. In fact they were very naughty indeed.

One day Pip broke the clothes line, and all the washing fell into the mud. Then Melia broke Mary's favourite teapot and she wouldn't say she was sorry. And Roundy flew into a temper and pulled Mary's whiskers.

*53*

Mary was dreadfully upset. She cried a big puddle of tears. Then she went upstairs to her room and packed her bag. She put on her hat and her coat. Then she wrote a goodbye letter and put it on her dressing table.

She slipped downstairs and went out of the front door without anyone seeing her. She went down the road and caught the bus at the corner.

Mummy and Daddy Doll were out visiting friends. When they came home, there was no Mary Mouse to open the door.

"Where is Mary Mouse?" Mummy Doll asked. The children didn't know. They called "Mary! Mary!" But no one came.

"Perhaps she is in her room and has gone to sleep," said Mummy Doll. So she went up to Mary's little bedroom. All her belongings had gone. Mummy Doll saw the note that Mary had left on the dressing table. She picked it up and read it:

The children don't love me any more, so I am going away.
Mary

Mummy Doll went downstairs and told the children.

"I do love her, I do!" cried Melia, and burst into tears.

"I want her to come back!" said Pip. "I'm going to go out and look for her."

"I want Mary to put me to bed," wept little Roundy. "I won't pull her whiskers again."

"Oh dear," said Mummy Doll. "We must find someone else to look after you now."

So the next day a wooden doll came to look after the children and clean the house. Her name was Matilda and she was very strict indeed.

The three children were very unhappy. They got together in a corner and made up their minds to go and look for Mary. They put on their woolly hats and their coats and they set off down the road together.

Where should they go first? Melia remembered the story that Mary had told them about the Mouse family where she had lived before. So they went to find the mouse hole and knocked at the door.

Mother Mouse came to the door and asked them to come in. The room was very dirty and untidy. The curtains were torn and there was food left on the table. Father Mouse was sitting with his feet up on the hot stove. The room smelt

so much that Melia
held her nose.

"We are looking for Mary,"
said Pip. "Have you seen her?"

"Mary Mouse isn't here," said
Mother Mouse. "She was much
too clean and tidy for us, so we
sent her away. We don't want
her back. We like to be untidy."

The children felt very
sad. They left the mouse hole
and went to look for Teddy

the Bear, who knew Mary well.

"I don't know where she is," he said. "Let's go and ask Pom the Panda." But Pom the Panda hadn't seen Mary either.

"We'll go and ask Peter the Penguin," he said. But Peter hadn't seen Mary.

"We must go and ask Benny the Toy Cat," said Peter. But Mary wasn't there either. Then Teddy had to lend Melia his handkerchief because she cried so much.

"We'll take you home," said Pom. "Perhaps Mary Mouse will have come back."

But there was only Matilda, the wooden doll, at home, and she was angry. She chased their friends away with a broom. And then she put the poor children into a dark cupboard and locked the door.

Mummy and Daddy Doll were out, so nobody heard the children crying.

But wait — who is this creeping up to the window to look in? Surely it is Mary Mouse — come to see if the children are missing her . . .

"They are crying," she said. "Where are they? I must go and see."

Mary Mouse went into the house. There was Matilda, the wooden doll.

"Get out of my kitchen!" said Matilda.

"This is my kitchen," said Mary. "Where are my children?" She rushed to the cupboard and unlocked it. The children ran out crying. Oh, how pleased they were to see Mary again! How they hugged her!

"We love you, we love you! Come back and live with us and we will always be good!" they said.

Mary Mouse turned to the wooden doll.

"You can go, Wooden Doll," she said. "You have made my kitchen dirty and untidy. And you have been unkind to the children. Go at once." But the wooden doll wouldn't go. She stood and glared at Mary. So Mary picked up the broom and ran after Matilda, who ran away as fast as she could and did not come back.

Mummy and Daddy Doll were very pleased when they came home and found Mary there.

"I won't go away again," said Mary. "Cheer up, and I'll make you all some lovely ginger buns."

Then Pip made Mary Mouse a dear little stool to sit on. She was so pleased. Melia made her a big fat pin cushion with her name on it. And Roundy spent his Saturday pennies on a stick of peppermint and gave it to Mary.

Now everyone is happy again. Mary Mouse sat on the stool and sucked the peppermint, with the pin cushion on her knee.

# Chapter 8

# Jumpy and Whiskers

The winter
passed and
spring came.
One afternoon
Mary Mouse
took the three
children out for a
walk. They went into a wood to pick
primroses. Suddenly Melia heard a
dog whining loudly.

"Listen!" she cried. "There is a
little dog crying!"

They looked around to see where
the noise was coming from.

Under a bush, Mary found a little
round ball of white hair spotted with

black. He was trembling with fright and very thin.

"He must be a stray dog with no home, poor thing!" said Mary.

"Let's take him home," said Pip. "I'll carry him."

So they took him back to the little Doll's House and gave him some warm milk to drink.

"Shall we keep him?" Mummy Doll asked. The children all shouted "Yes!"

Pip fetched a box for the puppy to sleep in and Melia put a cushion into it. Roundy gave him his favourite ball, the one that bounced the best. Mary gave him a bowl with DOG written on it.

The puppy grew fat. He rushed about and was quite mad. The children named him Jumpy because he jumped so much. They loved him very much.

Jumpy went for walks with the

children. He was good company.
But he was often very naughty. Once
he chewed all the roses off Mary
Mouse's hat. Another time he ran off
with Daddy Doll's slippers, and hid
them in the oven. When Mary
Mouse found them, they were quite
cooked, and Daddy Doll was very
cross. He smacked Jumpy.

Once Jumpy stole a string of
sausages from the kitchen table. He
ran into the garden with them, and
bumped into Pip. The
sausages got tangled
round Pip's

legs and he fell down.

Then lots more dogs smelled the sausages and came into the garden. They tried to eat the sausages round Pip's legs, and poor Pip cried.

"The dogs are trying to eat me! Help me, help me!"

After that Daddy Doll smacked Jumpy so hard that he thought he had better be good. And so he was, and everybody was pleased with him. Mummy Doll bought him a blue ribbon to put round his neck.

One day Mary Mouse decided that it was time for spring cleaning. Daddy Doll said that he would paint the window frames outside the house. He went to get a plank and rested it on two ladders. Then he went to find his brushes.

While he was away, Pip thought that he would run along the plank. So he climbed one of the ladders and began to run along the plank. But his foot slipped and *Splash*! He fell right into the bucket of paint below. When Daddy Doll came back, he saw a funny little white thing running round the garden. He caught Pip and took him to Mary Mouse.

"That's what comes of being silly," said Mary, and popped Pip into a hot bath.

Then Melia thought that she would help to paper a wall. But Roundy got in the way, and oh dear! Somehow he got pasted to the wall . . . He did look funny wriggling behind the paper, and how he yelled!

"What dreadful children," said Mary Mouse. "I can't get any spring cleaning done!"

But it was not only the children who were a nuisance. Jumpy began to bark at the vacuum cleaner, and he put his nose down to sniff at it. In a second he found himself rushing

into the cleaner with the dust, and
into the dustbag. It took Mary
Mouse a long time to get him out.

At last she went to Mummy Doll.
"Please send the children and
Jumpy to their aunt," she said.

So Mummy Doll sent them off and
Mary Mouse was able to get on with
the spring cleaning. She banged all
the carpets as hard as she could, she
washed all the curtains and hung
them again fresh and clean. Then
she began to miss the children.

"I want them back," she said. So she went to fetch them. She took a big sweet for each of them. They were very pleased to see her and Jumpy licked her one hundred times.

Now the house looked lovely. But the garden was very untidy.

"I do wish we had a gardener," said Daddy Doll. "I can't look after it all myself."

So he put a notice in the newsagent:

GARDENER
WANTED FOR THE
DOLL'S HOUSE.

The next day a handsome young mouse arrived. His name was Whiskers. Everyone liked him, so he stayed and worked hard in the garden. He taught Pip how to dig well with his spade. He made Melia weed the flower beds carefully. He even let Roundy water the flower beds for him. But Roundy watered

Jumpy as well, and Jumpy didn't like it. He ran into the kitchen and shook himself hard, so that drops of water flew everywhere.

"Goodness!" said Mary. "I shall have to get an umbrella if you do that, Jumpy."

One day Whiskers planted a beautiful bed of flowers. But Jumpy came along and buried a bone in the very middle of it. He quite spoiled the bed and Whiskers was very angry with him.

He went to Daddy Doll.

"You must send that dog away," he said. "He is destroying the garden."

Daddy Doll was upset.

"Oh dear!" he said. "I suppose he will have to go."

The children were very sad. But Daddy Doll went to find a new home for Jumpy. Jumpy's tail was right

72

down all day long.

The day came for Jumpy to leave.
The children took him for one last
walk. As they went into the town,
Roundy's ball suddenly ran into the
road. Roundy ran after it — and
"Oh, look out Roundy! There's a car
coming!"

But before the car could knock
Roundy over, Jumpy leapt at him
and caught him by the seat of his
trousers and carried him out of the
way.

Everyone cheered Jumpy,
and when Mummy Doll heard what
had happened she was very glad.

"We can't possibly let Jumpy go
away now," she said.

So he stayed, and Whiskers Mouse
made him promise never to bury
bones in the garden beds again.

## Chapter 9

# Mary Mouse Gets Married

The
time came
for the cherries to ripen on the tree
in the garden. One day Whiskers
took out the ladder and climbed
up to pick the cherries.
But his foot slipped and
he fell to the ground.

He lay on the grass and groaned. Mary Mouse came running out. She helped him indoors and put him in her own little bed and nursed him. She had to sleep in the kitchen chair but she didn't mind. While Whiskers was in bed, the children worked hard in the garden. And when he was better, he took Mary Mouse's hand, and said:

"You are so good and kind, Mary Mouse. Please will you marry me?"

"Oh, no!" said Mary. "I couldn't possibly leave the children."

"There is a cellar below the kitchen," Whiskers replied. "We could live there."

"Oh yes," said Mary. "Then I should be near the children all the time." And she went to tell Mummy Doll.

"You see," she said, "mice like a hole to live in. I could make a very nice home there."

"Of course you may have the cellar," said Mummy Doll. "Let's go and have a look at it."

When the children heard that Whiskers and Mary Mouse were to get married, they were most excited.

"I shall make you a chair for a wedding present," said Pip, and he began work at once.

"I shall sew you a beautiful table cloth with MM in the corner," said

Melia.

"And I shall paint you a lovely picture of my engine," said Roundy, and he got out his paints.

"I shall give you my biggest bone," said Jumpy. "It's a bit smelly, but very nice!"

"I shall paint the cellar door and put a knocker and a bell on it," said Daddy Doll.

"I shall give you plenty of brushes and brooms to keep your house tidy," said Mummy Doll.

Melia sat at her desk and wrote out all the wedding invitations in her best writing.

The postman delivered all the invitations. There was one for Teddy the Bear, one for Peter the Penguin. And one each for Benny the Cat and Pom the Panda. And there were invitation cards for all Mary Mouse's own family.

Mary's mother, Mrs Mouse, was

very pleased. "We shall all have to buy new clothes," she said.

At last the wedding day came. Melia helped Mary Mouse to put on her beautiful wedding dress. Whiskers looked very handsome in his striped trousers and top hat.

The children all had new clothes. And the guests came in their best clothes too.

After the wedding everyone threw confetti at Mary and Whiskers, and it looked like a coloured snowstorm.

The wedding cake was magnificent. It had three layers and was as tall as Roundy. On the top were two little sugar mice dressed like Whiskers and Mary. Mary cut the cake carefully and everyone had a piece.

At last it was time to go. Whiskers and Mary went off on their honeymoon in a beautiful red toy car. They waved goodbye, and

Roundy cried.

"I don't want Mary to go away," he sobbed.

"She will come back," said Mummy Doll. "We shall have fun getting her house ready."

The next day they went down to the cellar. There was only one room. It had a sofa, a chair and a table. Roundy hung up his picture.

"I wish I could live here too," he said.

Melia put her cloth on Mary's table. And Pip brought his chair down.

They all missed Mary Mouse very much and the house soon began to look untidy. And in the garden the weeds grew faster than the flowers.

Then one day, Hurray! In at the gate came Mary and Whiskers. The children ran to meet them shouting, and Jumpy went mad with joy.

"Welcome home!" cried Daddy

and Mummy Doll. "Your mouse
hole is ready for you, Mary and
Whiskers."

Then in at the funny front door
beneath the kitchen went Mary and
Whiskers Mouse.

## Chapter 10

# Mary Mouse and her Children

Several weeks went by. Then one day Mary Mouse called the children.

"Come and see," she said. "I have something to show you. But you must be very quiet."

Melia, Pip and Roundy went into Mary's house on tiptoe. There in a big cradle, they saw six little baby mice, all with pointed noses.

"These are my children," said Mary. "They are one day old." A baby mouse sat up and squeaked. "That one's Squeaker!" said Mary.

Melia, Pip and Roundy were each allowed to nurse two of the baby mice. Then they watched Mary give them their bath.

Pip and Melia helped to give them their bottles and Roundy rocked the cradle.

The next night there was such an upset. One of the baby mice had gone! Mary was in tears.

"Where has my little Squeaker gone? I've looked everywhere!"

And where do you think he was? Roundy had taken him to bed and there they were tucked up together, fast asleep!

Melia sometimes took the six babies out in the pram. Everyone stopped to look at them.

They grew very fast, and soon ran all over the place. There were three boys and three girls. The boys were called Frisky, Scamper and Squeaker and the girls were called Woffly, Patter and Tiny.

Mary dressed them all very nicely.

One day Squeaker and Roundy sailed paper boats on the bath and they let the water overflow. It dripped through onto Daddy Doll's head. He was very angry.

Then, when Melia left the larder door open, the three girl mice crept in and nibbled the cheese and the bacon. Mummy Doll was angry.

And then Squeaker and Pip got into trouble. They fell into the cucumber frame and broke the glass and spoiled the cucumbers that Whiskers was growing.

"It is time the children went to school," said Mary Mouse. So she went to see Mr Chalk. He was a toy monkey who kept the school. He

looked very grand and strict. He had plenty of pupils in his school. There was a clockwork mouse, a toy kitten with a long tail and green eyes, a toy lamb and three baby ducks.

When the six little mice arrived, Mr Chalk received them kindly and shook hands with them and smiled a nice monkey smile.

Back in the Doll's House Melia, Pip and Roundy missed the baby mice very much. When they came home and proudly showed the children their new books and pencils, Melia and Pip ran to Mummy Doll.

"We want to go to school, too!" they said. So the next day the six baby mice set off for school, and Pip and Melia went too. Poor Roundy was left at home by himself. He cried loudly.

"You are too little to go to school," said Mummy Doll hugging him.

"I shall be a naughty boy till you let me go!" said bad little Roundy, stamping his foot. And he was naughty. He took the flowers out of the vase and threw them on the floor.

He broke Mummy Doll's best teapot.
It smashed into a hundred pieces.
Then he spilt ink on the carpet.

"I want to go to school!" he
shouted. "Let me go!"

That day Squeaker came home
crying. Roundy put his arm round
him.

"What's happened? Tell me."

"Where's Mummy?" sobbed
Squeaker. "I don't want to go to
school any more."

"Well now," said Mary Mouse
crossly. "Here is Roundy begging to
go to school and you are
begging not to."

"I didn't know how
to spell 'cat'," wept Squeaker.
"So Mr Chalk made me stand
in the corner".

"Oh dear!" said Roundy. "I don't
know how to spell 'cat' either. Will
I have to stand in the corner too?"
After that Roundy decided to stay at
home until he could spell 'cat'. And
he was very good indeed. He picked
Mummy Doll some more flowers and
even scrubbed the ink stain in the
carpet.

Melia was very good at school. She
was always top of the class. Pip was
lazy. He often stood in the corner.
All the little mice were good except
Squeaker. One day he drew a
naughty picture of Mr Chalk on the
blackboard.

"You shall have top marks for
drawing," said Mr Chalk. "But I
must punish you for being cheeky."

The three baby ducks tried hard

to be good. But whenever it rained, they went out of the classroom and paddled in the puddles and wouldn't come in.

The clockwork mouse was sometimes naughty, but as he ran very fast, Mr Chalk could not catch him. But one day Mr Chalk took away his key, and after that the clockwork mouse could only run when Mr Chalk wound him up, so he had to be good.

The Toy Kitten teased the little mice.

"When I grow into a cat I shall chase you," she said. But Pip tied her tail to the chair, and wouldn't undo it until she promised not to grow up.

The end of the term arrived. It was time for a concert. Mary and Whiskers Mouse came. And Daddy and Mummy Doll brought Roundy. Melia danced on the tips of her toes.

Squeaker recited 'Hickory Dickory Dock'. The three baby ducks did a waddle dance, keeping perfect time. All the others performed a play.

After the concert Mr Chalk gave out the prizes. Melia got the prize for the best pupil. Squeaker got the prize for reciting. And the three ducks got the swimming prize. Pip got one for sums. And the Clockwork Mouse got one for running fast — and Mr Chalk gave him back his key. Everyone took their prizes home proudly.

"I haven't got a prize," said Roundy sadly.

"I shall give you a prize for being such a good boy," said Mary Mouse.

And now it is time for the holidays. Have a lovely time, everybody!

Also in this

series

Book 2  Mary Mouse goes to sea
Book 3  Mary Mouse and the caravan
Book 4  Mary Mouse goes up in a balloon

£2.50
each